MW01110131

Danny's Bean Plant

written and photographed
by
Mia Coulton

On Monday,

Danny saw little beans

on the table.

The beans were

too hard to eat.

On Tuesday,

the beans were in a cup

with water.

On Wednesday,
the water was gone
and the beans were fat.

On Thursday,

the beans were under

a wet paper towel.

On Friday,

Danny looked at the beans.

The wet beans
had changed again.

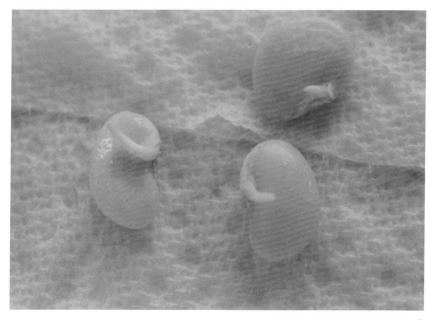

On Saturday,
the beans were hidden
in a jar full of dirt.

On Sunday,

the jar looked the same

as it did the day before.

Danny kept checking

the jar every day.

Then one day,

he saw green popping

out of the dirt.

He saw more and more

green each day.

Something was growing!

It was a bean plant!